LILY

TO THE rescue

DOG
DOG GOOSE

ALSO BY W. BRUCE CAMERON

W. BRUCE CAMERON

LILY
TO THE rescue

DOG
DOG GOOSE

Illustrations by
JENNIFER L. MEYER

A TOM DOHERTY ASSOCIATES BOOK
NEW YORK

LILY TO THE RESCUE: DOG DOG GOOSE

Copyright © 2020 by W. Bruce Cameron
Illustrations © 2020 by Jennifer L. Meyer

A Starscape Book
Published by Tom Doherty Associates
120 Broadway
New York, NY 10271

www.tor-forge.com

The Library of Congress Cataloging-in-Publication Data
is available upon request.

ISBN 978-1-250-23452-0 (trade paperback)
ISBN 978-1-250-23451-3 (hardcover)
ISBN 978-1-250-23450-6 (ebook)

Our books may be purchased in bulk for promotional, educational, or business use. Please contact your local bookseller or the Macmillan Corporate and Premium Sales Department at 1-800-221-7945, extension 5442, or by email at MacmillanSpecialMarkets@macmillan.com.

First Edition: September 2020

Printed in the United States of America

0 9 8 7 6 5 4

228 3994

Dedicated to the wonderful people helping animals at
Wayside Waifs in Kansas City.

LILY
TO THE rescue

DOG
DOG GOOSE

1

I am a dog, and my name is Lily. I have a girl, and her name is Maggie Rose.

Today Maggie Rose put me on a leash. That meant I was going someplace exciting!

I trotted on my leash beside Maggie Rose. Craig walked with us. He is Maggie Rose's much older brother, and from where I stand, he looks very tall. Maggie Rose has another brother named Bryan, but he is not as tall, and he was not walking with us today.

My job when I am walking with Maggie Rose is to look for things that she might not notice, such as a squirrel who needs to be chased, or bushes where dogs have lifted their legs.

"Know what kind of ice cream cone you want, Maggie Rose?" Craig asked while I was busy sniffing one of those bushes.

"Strawberry, because it's pink. Pink's my favorite color," Maggie replied.

"I thought you liked vanilla ice cream with sprinkles on it," Craig objected.

Maggie Rose frowned. "That was last year, when I was in second grade. I'm a third-grader now, so I like strawberry."

Craig nodded. "Makes sense."

A car drove past us on the street. A dog had his head out the window, and he barked at me. I knew what he was trying to tell me: "I'm in the car and you're not! I'm in the car and you're not!"

He kept barking until the car turned a corner. Some dogs are like that. They start barking and then they just don't stop, even if they have forgotten why they were barking in the first place. I am a well-behaved dog, and I do not do such things.

We walked a little more, and then Craig went inside a building while I stayed outside with Maggie Rose. In a little while, Craig was back. He was carrying an ice cream cone in each hand, which I thought was a wonderful thing to do!

They sat at a table, and I did Sit. I am extremely good at Sit. I was sure that when Maggie Rose noticed what an incredible Sit I was doing, I would get some of that ice cream. Nothing else would even make sense.

But then a loud, deep voice startled us all. "Go away!" a man shouted.

We all jumped. I looked over my shoulder. There was a parking lot behind us, and a man was standing at the edge of it, looking angrily into a little stretch of trees and bushes. "Go away!" he shouted again.

"Whoa," Craig said. "It's Mr. Swanson! You know, he lives two houses down." He raised his voice a little. "What's going on, Mr. Swanson?"

Mr. Swanson turned around to look at us. He walked up to our table and pointed one thumb over his shoulder. "Hi, kids. See the fox?"

Craig shook his head. "What fox?" said Maggie Rose.

Mr. Swanson pointed into the trees. "There. Right there. See it?"

We all looked into the woods. I lifted my nose, and I caught a scent that was new to me. It was like a male dog, but different— wilder and more fierce. I pulled on my leash a little, so that Maggie Rose would let me go and meet this new animal. We could play together!

I am very good at playing with other animals. I often go to a place called Work and play with all the animals there. Work is where Mom spends most of her time helping animals. She calls Work "the rescue."

Maggie Rose twitched. "I see it! Lily, do you see it? See the fox?"

That was a new word to me—"fox." It must be the name of the animal.

The fox was crouched behind a bush, so I could only catch a glimpse of short fur and bright eyes and ears that stood up in stiff triangles. He stared at us hard.

"He's here for the eggs," Mr. Swanson said.

"What eggs?" Maggie Rose asked.

"Come on, I'll show you."

Mr. Swanson took us toward a big wooden box in the middle of the parking lot. It had some bushes and flowers growing inside it.

"A goose laid some eggs right in this planter," Mr. Swanson said. "But a couple of days ago, some men were here fixing potholes in the parking lot, and I guess the noise scared her. She flew away and never came back."

"Oh no," said Maggie Rose.

When we reached the wooden box, Maggie Rose looked into it. She gasped.

Craig peered over her shoulder. "Whoa, look at that!"

"Well, now," Mr. Swanson said. "That's remarkable!"

I put my front feet on the edge of the wooden box so that I could see inside. There was something moving in there!

Actually, there were a lot of somethings. They were small and fuzzy, like the kittens I play with at Work sometimes. But they also had beaks, like my friend Casey the crow. (Casey spent some time at Work because Mom needed to help his wing, so we got to know each other really well.) They huddled together in a group making tiny peeping noises. Broken eggshells were all around them.

"The eggs hatched!" exclaimed Maggie Rose. "They're so cute!"

"They're cute, all right," Craig said. He didn't sound as happy as Maggie Rose did. "But where's their mom?"

"Hasn't been back since she flew off," Mr. Swanson said, shaking his head.

"Let's put Lily in the planter with the baby geese," Maggie Rose suggested. "She will protect them from the fox."

At the word "fox" I turned to smell for the animal in the woods, but it had run off without even trying to be friends. I thought that was very unfriendly. Life would be better if all animals acted more like dogs.

Maggie Rose picked me up. "They must be scared without their mom."

"They're going to be even more scared if a dog's in there with them," Mr. Swanson warned her.

"Actually, my sister might be right," Craig answered.

"Lily helps out at the rescue all the time,"

Maggie Rose explained to Mr. Swanson. "She plays with all the animals."

"If you say so," Mr. Swanson replied doubtfully.

Maggie Rose put me inside the big wooden box. "Be nice to the baby geese, Lily," she told me.

2

I stood still and waited. I have learned that new animals don't always like it if I rush at them and sniff their butts, which is the polite way to get to know one another for dogs. Sometimes they need time to understand that I just want to play.

Not these little creatures, though. They rushed toward me. It was funny! They didn't pounce like kittens, and they didn't fly like grownup birds, and they didn't run like

puppies. They moved in their own way, with a waddle.

I put my nose down to sniff them. They smelled very interesting—fluffy and feathery and young. They clustered around my muzzle and nibbled on my whiskers with their tiny beaks. It didn't hurt. They were too small to hurt anybody. They really seemed to like me!

"Well, would you look at that," Mr. Swanson

said. "It's like they understand why you put your dog in there with them!"

"It's kind of amazing," Craig agreed. "I've seen Lily play with kittens and grumpy old dogs and a ferret and even a crow."

"So now she's friends with the baby geese!" my girl exclaimed happily.

"Goslings," Craig replied.

"Huh?"

"Baby geese are called goslings."

"Goslings," Maggie Rose repeated. "Goslings."

I heard that word, goslings. I decided the tiny birds were goslings. That's why Maggie Rose and Craig kept saying it.

"Don't know what to feed them," Mr. Swanson said. "I could bring some water, I guess. But I don't know where to get goose milk."

Craig laughed. Maggie Rose smiled a little.

"They're birds, not mammals, Mr. Swanson," she explained. "They don't drink milk."

"Oh, right," Mr. Swanson said. "I wasn't thinking straight. Fact is, I was thinking about my wife."

"About Mrs. Swanson?" Maggie Rose asked.

Mr. Swanson nodded. "She's goose-crazy, to tell you the truth. Anything with a picture of a goose on it, she'll buy it. She's got a collection of goose eggs. She'd have geese of her own if she could, but I'm allergic to their feathers. Can't even wear a down jacket. I wondered for a while if she'd pick geese over me, but so far she's stuck with me. But I bet she won't if she finds out I let anything happen to these little fellas."

"That fox will get them for sure if the mom doesn't come back," Craig said. "We better ask Mom and Dad what to do."

Mr. Swanson nodded. "That's right, I forgot—your mother runs that animal rescue." He dug in his back pocket. "Here, use my phone."

Craig took the phone. Human beings seem to like phones a lot. They stare at them and touch them and talk to them all the time, even with a dog in the room. I do not know why. Phones do not smell at all interesting.

"Good dog," Maggie Rose said. She took a bite of her ice cream. I stared at it unhappily—it was almost gone!

Craig had stopped talking to the phone. "Mom'll be here in a minute," he said. His ice cream *was* gone!

So apparently it was the part of the day where a good dog who wasn't getting any ice cream was supposed to stay in a box with a bunch of baby birds called goslings. I nudged a few of them aside and lay down and at once they were huddled all around me, trying to cuddle right up to my nose. I was worried that if I yawned they might try to climb into my mouth!

"Good, gentle girl," Maggie Rose praised. I heard a car pull up near us in the parking lot, and moments later I smelled Mom standing next to my girl. I wagged my tail very gently, so Mom would know I was glad to see her but I wouldn't knock any baby birds out of the box.

"Oh boy," Mom said, looking down at me.

"What's wrong, Mom?" Craig asked.

"Lily's protecting the goslings," my girl said proudly.

"I see that. And that's probably going to be a problem."

"Why?"

"Mr. Swanson," Mom asked, "when was the last time you saw the mother goose?"

"At least two days ago," Mr. Swanson said.

Mom shook her head. "Two days? That's too long. If the mom was going to come back, she'd have been here by now. And no sign of the father at all?"

"Never seen more than one goose by the nest," Mr. Swanson said.

"Well, the father would have been nearby, but you might not have seen him. He'd be keeping an eye on the nest, but out of sight, so he wouldn't attract predators."

"So they're not coming back?" Maggie Rose asked.

"Probably not," Mom said.

"Why did you say there's a problem, Mom?" Craig pressed.

"See, geese are imprinting birds," Mom said.

"Printing?" Mr. Swanson repeated, puzzled.

"Not printing. *Im*printing."

Maggie Rose's forehead wrinkled. "What does that mean?"

"When goslings hatch, they can't do much of anything for themselves," Mom explained. "So the very first thing they do is look around for their mother. Usually she's right there, sitting on the nest. But if she's gone for some reason, then the babies will decide that whatever animal they see first must be their mom. They'll follow that animal everywhere, and learn how to behave from it."

"Uh-oh," Maggie Rose said.

"There's no way either of you could have

known. Lily has been so good at helping our rescued animals feel welcome and safe. So naturally, you put her in the planter to calm the goslings. You didn't know about imprinting.

"It's unusual for geese to imprint on a dog, but it's happened," Mom continued. "And there's no way that I know of to change it."

"So the babies think Lily is their mother?" my girl asked. "And they think Lily's going to teach them how to be geese?"

Mom nodded. "Yes, exactly."

3

Mom pulled a small crate out of the back of the car. Then she reached for a handful of goslings. They were frightened, and they peeped and tried to dart away. I didn't move—I've learned that when animals are scared, it helps for me to lie still.

"Quick, everybody!" Mom urged.

Craig and Mr. Swanson both reached in to pick up goslings. "They're so light!" Craig said. "It's like holding air!"

Mr. Swanson managed to snag only one. "They're quick little things!" he said.

Maggie Rose didn't try to pick up any of the goslings. Instead, she picked *me* up.

"Take care of them, Lily," she said, and she put me inside the crate, too. The crate with the birds and me went into the car.

I have been in lots of crates. The first time I didn't like it, because it kept me apart from Maggie Rose. But I have learned not to mind. My girl always lets me out again in time, and meanwhile it is cozy to curl up and have a nap.

That's what I did. As the car started moving, I carefully checked to make sure there were no goslings beneath me, and lay down.

Peep! A high-pitched noise came from under my belly. I looked down in surprise to see a fuzzy little gosling wiggling out from underneath me. I must have missed one!

I gave it a lick and it wiggled its head and peeped some more.

We drove a little way, and then we stopped at Work.

I love Work!

Work is where so many of my friends live. There is Brewster the old dog, and sometimes Freddy the ferret comes to visit, and lots of cats and kittens and now and then a squirrel. We even had a couple of baby pigs once! There is always someone to play with at Work, though this would be the first time we had a whole flock of baby birds.

Mom carried the crate with the goslings and me inside the building. They seemed scared at the way the crate floor tilted and swung, staring at me as if expecting me to do something about it. All they did was peep, though—the same noise they'd been making the whole time.

Mom set my crate down in a larger pen, the kind that is called a kennel. Maggie Rose came inside the kennel, too.

Mom opened up the crate. The goslings stayed inside, huddled close to me, peeping.

"Call Lily," Mom said softly to Maggie Rose. "I bet if she comes out, the goslings will, too."

My girl called my name, and I went to her because I am a good dog. The goslings followed me out of the crate. They looked around the kennel and peeped in confusion.

"Okay," Mom said. She reached over to rub my ears and I leaned into it, groaning a little. "You can let Lily out of the kennel. I'll go get some goose food."

Mom left the room and Maggie Rose slipped me out of the kennel and closed the gate. I heard the goslings peeping very loudly behind me.

I wandered over to Brewster's kennel and whined at Maggie Rose until she let me in.

Brewster was curled up on his blanket in a corner. He lifted his head when I trotted in and sniffed him. Brewster is a friend of mine, even though he does not like to spend much time playing Chase-Me or I've-Got-the-Ball or Tug-on-a-Stick. He is old and prefers napping over playing.

Brewster smelled like food, and like the blanket he lay on, and like himself. He also smelled a lot like Bryan.

Bryan did not come to get ice cream with us. Brewster's fur smelled like Bryan most days. That was funny, because Brewster lived at Work and Bryan lived at Home. Why would Bryan's scent be on Brewster? Were they napping together?

By now the goslings were making so much noise that Brewster groaned. He gave me a look as if this were somehow all my fault, which was ridiculous.

"Lily! Lily, come!" Maggie Rose was kneeling next to the kennel with the goslings inside.

I hurried away from Brewster. When I reached my girl, the goslings rushed over to strain against the wire of the kennel, sticking their beaks out and peeping at me with their tiny voices.

Mom came back in the room, carrying a box. "I could hear them all the way from the supply kitchen," she remarked.

"They seem really upset that Lily is out and they're not. But I knew you would want them to stay in the kennel; they were so hard to catch the first time."

"Oh, I think they'll stick right by your dog no matter what," Mom replied.

I wagged at the word "dog."

"Open the kennel," Mom suggested.

Maggie Rose reached over to the kennel door and opened it up.

"Come on out, baby geese," she said.

4

The baby birds poured out of the kennel and frantically rushed over to me as if they hadn't been able to see I was right there the whole time. They tried to climb up onto me and fell off onto the floor and peeped and struggled to their feet again for another try. My girl stood up so they wouldn't try to climb on her, which was only right—I am Maggie Rose's dog, and if anyone was going to climb up on her, it should be me.

"Good dog, Lily," she told me.

I didn't even look up, because I'd been called "good dog" a lot lately, but before there had been no ice cream and I could smell there were no treats now.

Mom put the box that she was carrying down onto the floor and I went to examine it, the geese right on my heels. Inside it were seeds and pieces of grass and some small berries. Why bother to put stuff like that in a box?

The goslings seemed to be very interested in the box, though. Its sides were very low and they could climb right into it. They began waddling among the grass and seeds and berries, pecking and nibbling and peeping.

The things in that box were bird treats, then? I did not understand this at all. I'd done Come and Sit for Maggie Rose, but the little geese had not done anything except peep and climb all over me like I was a bird bed.

I padded over to a bowl of water and drank. Then, with a long, weary sigh, I flopped down on the floor and stretched out on my side for a nap like old Brewster.

Peep peep peep! Goslings instantly rushed over to surround me.

It seemed that these geese wanted to be really, really good friends with me! They nestled around me, huddling into my fur, pecking lightly at my skin.

"I think Lily will have to stay the night," Mom said. "The goslings won't be able to settle down without her."

"Can I stay, too?" Maggie Rose asked. "I can sleep on the couch."

Mom shook her head. "No, because Lily will want to lie with you, and the goslings will want to lie with her, and you'll end up sleeping with baby geese. You might roll over and crush them. Nope, I'm afraid Lily is going to have to handle her job as the new mother goose all by herself."

My girl's shoulders slumped. "I am going to miss my dog."

"I'm sure she'll miss you, too," Mom replied, "but if we separate her from them, it might make the goslings really, really upset."

There was some more talking, and after a while Maggie Rose brought me a whole bowl of food all for myself. I had to shake goslings off to eat it, and they peeped at me until I lay back down so they could snuggle beside me again.

This was getting to be ridiculous. I was

very much looking forward to going Home so I could sleep with my girl.

Except *that's not what happened*. Maggie Rose put me inside the goslings' kennel and left me there and went away!

I barked a little to remind her that she had forgotten me, but she didn't come back. I whined a few times, but that didn't work, either. Meanwhile the baby birds stared up at me as if I was waving an ice cream cone around. *What did they want?*

Brewster groaned and got up and circled around and lay back down, and as he did so he gave me a weary look, probably thinking I looked very silly with a bunch of goslings clinging to me.

Slowly the room got darker, although a little light still came in through a window. I sighed. A few goslings peeped. Then everything was quiet for a while, until something went *click*.

It was a door. The door was opening.

Someone came through the door, someone who smelled familiar. It was Bryan.

Bryan came into the room where I was in the kennel with the goslings. He was carrying the long stick that he sometimes uses to hit balls. He put the stick and a ball and a

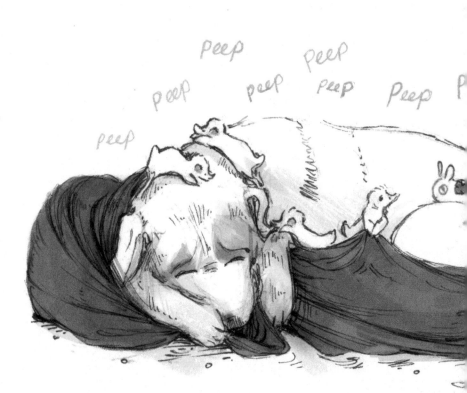

big leather glove down by the wall. Then he came over to my kennel.

He unlatched the door and looked in. "Lily, is that you?" he asked. "What are you doing with all those ducks?" He opened my kennel door.

I wagged my tail but didn't get up because I had all these peeping geese sticking to me. Bryan shrugged and kept moving. He stopped in front of Brewster's kennel.

"Hi, boy," I heard him say.

Bryan opened up the kennel door and Brewster actually climbed to his feet. Bryan pulled some treats out of his pocket and gave them to Brewster.

Okay, I was a good dog, too, just like Brewster. I got up, shaking off goslings, and left the kennel to go over to Bryan and Brewster.

The goslings followed me,

of course. They probably thought they were dogs, but that was just silly. Dogs know how to do Sit and Stay and Lie Down and Roll Over, and that is why they get treats. Other animals don't do these things, and that's why treats are not for them.

Well, every now and then cats get treats. But they don't really deserve them.

Bryan understood. He gave me a treat and did not give any to the goslings. I loved Bryan. Also, his hands smelled a little like peanut butter, and I love peanut butter.

Bryan sat down on the floor and leaned his back up against one wall of the kennel. Brewster lay down next to him and put his head in Bryan's lap. Bryan rubbed his ears and stroked his head, and Brewster let out a long groan of happiness.

"You're a good dog," Bryan whispered. "A good, good dog."

They stayed like that for a while. I did Sit

in case Bryan had any more treats hidden in his pockets. The goslings clustered around my feet and settled down. Brewster looked away, embarrassed for me.

After a while, Bryan sighed. "I have to go now," he said. Very gently, he picked up Brewster's head and put it on the ground. "Sorry, boy. I'll be back."

Then with a loud noise we heard the side door open. "Lily!"

It was my girl! She came rushing into the room of kennels and halted in surprise when she saw her brother in the kennel with Brewster's head in his lap.

"Bryan?" she said.

"Don't tell Mom," he whispered urgently.

5

I was greeting Maggie Rose with licks and wags while the goslings milled around underfoot, as if they didn't understand how wonderful it was that my girl had come back.

"What are you doing here, Bryan?" Maggie Rose asked.

"Maggie Rose, are you talking to me?" Mom called from another room at Work.

"Um . . . I am here with Lily!" my girl called back.

I wagged at my name.

Bryan stood up. Brewster did Sit at his feet.

"I'm just visiting Brewster," Bryan explained quietly.

"But it's after dinner," Maggie Rose said.

"So what? I can't pet a dog after dinner?"

"You told Mom and Dad you were playing baseball with your friends!"

"Yeah, well." Bryan looked embarrassed.

I lay down and rolled over, and the baby birds scattered when my girl started rubbing my tummy.

"You play baseball with your friends every night!" Maggie Rose went on.

"No, I don't," Bryan said. "I come to visit Brewster after dinner every night."

"You do?" Maggie Rose stopped rubbing my tummy. She straightened up and the goslings all rushed to be with me even though I had been lying here the whole time. I wearily got to my feet and did Sit like Brewster.

"He's all by himself. All night long," Bryan said. "I just . . . visit him. That's all. Don't tell anybody, Maggie Rose!"

My girl's eyes widened. "You should adopt Brewster!" she said.

Bryan made a snorting kind of noise. I looked at him in surprise. Humans don't usually snort.

"Mom would never let me," he said. "You know her and her rules—our family can't adopt animals from the Rescue because it sets a bad example, somehow."

"They let me have Lily," Maggie Rose pointed out.

"That's different. That's because you're the youngest," Bryan said. "And they love Craig because he's the oldest and responsible and stuff. But they're not going to let *me* have a dog. There's no point even asking."

"Except Brewster is a senior dog. Mom says it is really hard to place an old dog with a new family," Lily argued.

Brewster and I both wagged at "dog" but the goslings didn't react at all. They were still staring at me as if I were a human with bird treats in my pocket.

Bryan didn't say anything. The goslings poked their beaks into my fur.

"What if you paid the adoption fee?" Maggie Rose suggested suddenly.

Bryan snorted again. Brewster and I glanced at each other. I wondered if Bryan was going to be making this noise all the time now.

"I don't have anywhere near that much money," he replied. "It's, like, two hundred dollars."

"But if you did," Maggie Rose insisted, "I'll bet you Mom would say yes."

"Whatever. It's way more than I have."

"But I have money, too," Maggie Rose pointed out.

Bryan stared at her. Brewster flopped down on the floor with a groan. I didn't, because if I did I would be swarmed with goslings.

"I'll give you all my money," Maggie Rose continued. "And then we can do extra chores around the house to earn more. If you had the adoption fee, Mom would have to say yes!"

"You would do that for me?"

"For you and for Brewster."

Brewster had been snoozing, but he opened a lazy eye when my girl said his name.

"Okay!" Bryan replied.

"Maggie Rose?" called a voice from the door to the yard. "I'm done closing up for the night—time to go home. Say bye to Lily."

It was Mom's voice. Bryan made a face at Maggie Rose and held a finger in front of his lips. Maggie Rose nodded at him. He turned to leave through the front door.

"Bryan?" my girl said softly.

Bryan turned back.

"Mom and Dad do love you," Maggie Rose proclaimed. "And so do I."

Bryan snorted. *Again.*

I don't think I understood that my girl was going to leave me at Work so the baby birds could all try to climb on my head, and do it the next day, and the next, and the next.

Had I been a bad dog? Why wasn't I sleeping on my girl's bed?

The geese were with me constantly. They trailed along the floor behind me. They nibbled on my fur and wiggled under my belly. They nestled up close to me as soon as I stopped moving.

Why couldn't they climb on Brewster instead? All he did was lie there. He would make an excellent bird's nest! But no, the goslings wanted to be with just me.

One morning my girl took me and the goslings out into the yard. I went through the dog door by myself, but Maggie Rose had to hold the people door open for the geese.

The yard at Work is a nice place, with grass and one tree with a squirrel who comes down to be chased every now and then. Today the squirrel was not around, though. Instead Craig was there, picking up some papers that had blown into the yard.

"Hey, they've gotten a little bigger already," Craig said.

I wanted to play Chase-Me or Fetch with Craig and Maggie Rose, but it was hard with the geese underfoot. The only game they seemed to know was Follow-Lily-Everywhere.

After a little while, Mom came into the yard with another lady who had been eating bacon for breakfast, which I appreciated very much.

"Oh, they are precious!" the new woman exclaimed, clapping her hands.

I thought maybe she wanted me to come and sniff her. Sometimes people who clap their hands want that. But she wasn't even looking at me. She was looking at the goslings.

"Hi, Mrs. Swanson," Maggie Rose said.

The new lady, I figured out, was called Mrs. Swanson. She liked to talk.

"I just love geese," she said to Mom and Maggie Rose and sort of to me and the goslings, too. "I always have. You know the way some people just love cats? I feel that way about geese. When my husband told me about these poor orphaned babies, I knew I had to come and see them."

The goslings were pecking at my feet. I turned around and nudged them out of the way with my nose so I could go and sniff Mrs. Swanson's shoes.

"Maybe I could help support them?" Mrs. Swanson asked Mom. "I'd love to help buy food for them."

Mom smiled. "We're always looking for donations to support our work," she said.

Mrs. Swanson talked some more and some more and then she and Mom went away. Maggie Rose grinned at me. "She's a little funny," she whispered. "Why would anybody like geese better than dogs, Lily?"

I crawled into her lap. The geese circled around, working up the nerve to climb up with me. Goslings do not always understand that sometimes a dog just wants to be with her girl.

Craig came over to see me but probably not the goslings. "Hey, good dog, Lily," he said, leaning in to talk to my girl.

"So," he murmured quietly. "I know something is going on, Maggie Rose."

6

I looked at my girl with interest—she had stiffened, and seemed worried.

"Something going on?" she repeated innocently.

"With you and Bryan. All of a sudden you're doing all these extra jobs around the house? Bryan was sweeping the garage—last time he did that it was because Dad was using it as *punishment*. I saw you straightening the shelves and dusting them. What gives? Did you two do something really bad?" Craig demanded.

"No-o-o," my girl answered slowly.

"Then what? Why are you two working so hard to impress Mom and Dad?"

"Okay, look Craig, if I tell you, you have to promise not to tell anyone else. Okay?"

Craig folded his arms. "You know what Dad always says—you can't make that promise until you know what it is. Like, what if you and Bryan robbed a bank or something? I'd have to tell."

My girl sighed. I thought about lying down on her feet, but I knew as soon as I did I'd be covered with baby birds. "Okay, I'll tell you."

"Good."

Maggie Rose took a deep breath. "Bryan and I robbed a bank."

"Maggie Rose!" Craig was laughing. "Come on."

"Well . . . you know how Mom always says Brewster is a senior dog that nobody will ever want and it's sad because he is so great but people don't adopt old pets?" My girl's words were coming out of her in a rush. "Well, Bryan does want to adopt Brewster!"

Craig was shaking his head. "You know Mom's policy about that. We can foster rescued animals, but if we adopt one that's foster failure, and it sets a bad example for the other people who foster."

"Yes," my girl said, "but she made an exception for me, because Lily is such a special dog. She'll do the same for Bryan—otherwise, it's not fair!"

"I guess it's not fair," Craig agreed, "but you know Mom. She'll come up with a reason that will make sense so she can be both fair and stick to the rules."

Maggie Rose nodded. "That's why Bryan and I are raising money to pay Brewster's adoption fee. If we have the fee, Mom has to say yes, doesn't she?"

Craig looked thoughtful. "You know, this could work. When you say it's not fair to let you have Lily but not let Bryan have Brewster, she'll probably say 'okay, but only if you pay the adoption fee'—because she knows you don't have that kind of money. How much do you have?"

"Almost half . . . of half," my girl admitted hesitantly.

The goslings were all clustered around my butt, as if they wanted me to sit on them. Which meant I couldn't sit, even though I wanted to!

"Okay, well . . . I've got some money saved up, so you guys can have that, too. But you still have a long way to go," Craig told her.

My girl pumped her fist and said "*Yes!*"—so happy to have a dog like me she nearly jumped.

I wish I could say that I went Home and the goslings stayed at Work that night, but instead I was left at Work with Brewster and the silly birds.

I stayed at Work for days and days. I did most of the things I usually did. I sniffed Brewster and my other friends and said hello to all the people who came to take care of the dogs and cats and squirrels and ferrets and birds and other animals who live there. I was a good dog, but I missed my girl at night and I was tired of being climbed on by geese.

Maggie Rose came to see me every day, though. Often she would let me and the goslings out into the yard. I would sniff and the geese would follow me, sometimes climbing over each other to be close to me. They were right there when I squatted.

I don't mind peeing in front of other dogs. But for some reason it is embarrassing to do it in front of baby geese.

Dad had set up a small plastic pool in the yard, and he was standing there filling it up with a hose. I went over and slurped up a drink. Water from a hose tastes different from water in a bowl.

The goslings followed, of course. I was willing to teach them to drink from the hose, but they weren't interested in that. They were focused on the water in the pool.

Dad put a long, flat piece of wood on the ground. One end of the wood was on the edge of the pool and the other was in the grass, so it made a ramp.

"Help them out, Maggie Rose," he said.

Maggie Rose knelt down. "Go on, Gertrude," she said, pushing a gosling up the ramp.

Dad chuckled. "Gertrude?"

"That's her name. She's the biggest,"

Maggie Rose said. "And she's the bravest, too. She does things first, and the rest follow. Okay, Mr. Waddle-puss. Fluffy. Goofy. Downy. Oh, and Harold. You go, too."

She shooed the goslings up the ramp.

When Gertrude reached the top of the ramp, she didn't hesitate. She plunged straight into the water. The other goslings followed her.

I know about water. It's good for drinking when it's in bowls or hoses, but if you try to stand on it or run on it, you go down to the bottom.

But for some reason this water was different! The goslings did not sink. They stayed right on the top, and when they paddled with their legs they moved over the water.

I put my feet up on the edge of the pool to watch this amazing sight. Gertrude paddled right over to me. The others followed. They peeped at me as if they wanted me to get in and swim, but swimming is for geese and not for dogs like me.

Some of them even ducked their bodies under the water. I whined and looked at Maggie Rose. But it turned out that I didn't need to worry. The goslings popped right back up.

"They know how to swim!" Maggie Rose exclaimed.

"Geese can swim at one day old," Dad said.

After that, the goslings swam in the pool every day. And every night I slept in the kennel with a bunch of geese burrowing into me. Brewster kept regarding them sourly, probably thinking I was a poor excuse for a dog with all these birds sitting on me.

Even worse than my embarrassment over being covered with geese was the fact that I was not with Maggie Rose. I missed my girl so much that I finally realized what I had to do:

I needed to escape from Work.

7

I began to watch very carefully as Mom and my girl left Work every day. They always went out the back door into the yard, which was at the end of a hall. There was a door to that hall, but they only shut it when they were leading dogs to the kennels. Otherwise, it was open. Which meant I could run down the hall and out the dog door. And then Mom always held the gate open for Maggie Rose.

When that gate was open, I would have my chance!

I almost felt like a bad dog, just thinking about bursting through that gate, but I was tired of always being covered in geese, and I belonged with my girl.

One day Craig came to watch the goslings swim. I poked at his leg with my nose to remind him that dogs are important, too. He scratched my ears. Bryan was using a loud machine to blow leaves around in the front yard, and Mrs. Swanson came out to be with us, though she still seemed more interested in the geese than in a good dog who could do Sit and Roll Over.

"I have a lot of fall eggs that I've collected over the years," Mrs. Swanson said to Maggie Rose and Craig. "Would you like to see them?"

Craig looked at Maggie Rose. Maggie Rose

nodded and got my leash and led me to the gate. We slipped out, shutting the geese into the yard. Then we all went on a walk, Maggie Rose and me and Mom and Craig and Mrs. Swanson, too. It felt so good not to have a bunch of birds stepping all over my feet!

We crossed the field and passed Home and walked down the street to a house I'd never been in. It smelled like Mr. and Mrs. Swanson.

We went into the garage. "I'm sorry, it's a little cluttered," Mrs. Swanson said. "I keep meaning to organize it."

"So many geese!" Maggie Rose said. She held my leash and turned from side to side.

"Geese Christmas ornaments. Geese plates," Craig said, looking around.

"Stuffed geese!" Maggie Rose said, pointing.

"Geese statues!" Craig said, pointing somewhere else.

"Kids! Don't be rude," Mom said sternly.

Mrs. Swanson laughed. "They're not

being rude in the least. They're quite right! I do love geese!"

Why were all the people saying "geese" so much? We had left the geese behind at Work. I could not smell any geese here.

"But my very favorite part of my collection is inside," Mrs. Swanson went on. "Come in and let me show you."

We went inside the house. Mrs. Swanson

led us over to a shelf high up on the wall. A row of eggs was lined up on it.

I know about eggs because Mom or Dad cracks them for breakfast, and if there are leftovers they sometimes end up in my bowl. I looked up at these eggs hopefully, but no one seemed to be thinking of a good dog in that moment.

"These are very rare," Mrs. Swanson explained.

"Why?" Craig asked. "Don't geese lay eggs all the time?"

"They aren't ordinary eggs," Mrs. Swanson said. "They're fall eggs. Most geese don't lay eggs until they're a year old, in the spring.

But every now and then a young goose will lay an egg in the fall, right before she migrates. The eggs don't hatch. But sometimes people have one for sale and I'll buy it. They're rare and they're special—the first eggs from a goose!"

They all looked at the eggs for a while and talked some more. I sat down and scratched one of my ears. Then the other one.

At last the people were done talking about geese. Mom and Craig and Maggie Rose and I left.

"I didn't want to ask Mrs. Swanson," Craig said, "but she's had those eggs for years, right? Why don't they stink?"

"If an egg never cracks, it won't stink," Mom said. "The water inside evaporates eventually, and the solid parts of the egg just stay there, dried up, forever."

"Goose mummies," Craig said. "Creepy!"

Maggie Rose squealed and Mom laughed

a little. "That's pretty much right," she said. "That's exactly what fall eggs are!"

"What's 'migrate,' Mom?" my girl asked.

"It's when they fly south for the winter," Craig volunteered.

Mom nodded. "Exactly right. Geese fly out to where it is warm to fatten up, and come back here in the spring. Except our little goslings think that a dog is their mommy. Who is going to teach them to fly? And how will they know where to go if they think they are supposed to spend the winter with a dog?"

Back home the goslings were so overjoyed at my return I had to just stand there and let them flap at me and climb up and prod me with their beaks. Later, I was not able to follow my girl and Mom out the back gate because Maggie Rose

fed Brewster and me and my face was in the bowl, frantically licking up every scrap, and then I bolted for the dog door but Mom was already shutting the gate.

So I was just lying there at night, covered in birds, Gertrude huddled closest, Bryan

sitting with Brewster's head in his lap, when I heard a door open.

I lifted my head and sniffed. It was not Maggie Rose coming. It was Dad.

"Bryan?" he called.

Brewster and I both lifted our heads, startled, when Bryan made an alarmed-sounding noise. Dad came into the room. He stopped when he saw Bryan and Brewster.

"Bryan?" Dad said again.

8

Brewster and I could tell something was going on, and the goslings couldn't. Bryan and Dad were both tense. Brewster sat up but I didn't, because if I did the geese would start peeping in confusion and who could put up with that?

"So this is where you've been going every night. I thought you were playing ball with your friends," Dad said. "I went by the park, though, and you weren't there. Maggie Rose told me

I could find you here."

Bryan muttered something.

It sounded like "not any good."

"What?" Dad asked.

"They won't let me play," Bryan said, staring down at Brewster's head. "I'm not good enough."

Dad frowned. "What do you mean? You do fine with Craig and me."

Bryan shrugged. "I can't hit the ball."

"Well," Dad said. "Let's see about that. Come on, out in the yard."

"Now?" Bryan asked. He sounded surprised.

"Now," Dad said. "Get your bat and come on."

Dad headed out for the yard. Bryan eased Brewster's head off his lap and picked up his big stick and headed after Dad.

Brewster got up and shook himself and followed. I followed Brewster and Bryan. The goslings followed me.

Of course.

We went out in the backyard and Bryan and Dad started playing a game I have seen before. It's called Hit-a-Ball-With-a-Stick-So-Lily-Can-Chase-It.

Dad threw the ball and Bryan swung the

stick. But he missed the ball. It thudded into the grass.

I knew what to do! I ran after the ball. The goslings ran after me. Brewster sat and watched us all.

Bryan got to the ball before I did, so he won that time.

"Again," Dad said. Bryan threw the ball back to him. They tried this game a few more times. Each time Bryan swung his stick, he missed the ball. Each time he got to pick it up before I did, which wasn't as much fun as the other way around. Bryan seemed to feel the same way.

"See?" he said to Dad. His shoulders slumped. His voice was low.

"I do see," Dad replied. "You're looking at the wrong thing."

"Huh?" Bryan asked.

"You watch the ball when I throw it, but as

you swing, you change to looking at the bat. Keep your eye on the ball."

Bryan threw the ball to Dad. Dad threw it back. Bryan swung the stick again.

He hit the ball! Now we were really playing. The ball sailed toward the fence. I ran after it. The goslings ran after me. And then something amazing happened. Something I had never seen before.

Brewster ran. He heaved himself up and lumbered across the yard. He wanted the ball! It hit the fence and bounced off, right at him, and he scooped it up!

I stopped running. Gertrude thumped into my rump. The other goslings piled into her.

Brewster had gotten to the ball first!

But he didn't understand how to play this game at all. When you get the ball, you are supposed to run around the yard with it so that people chase you. Brewster just trotted back to Dad and put the ball down gently at his feet.

"Good dog," Dad said to Brewster.

What is good about forgetting to be chased?

Dad picked up the ball and threw it back to Bryan. Bryan hit it with the stick again.

"Hey!" Bryan exclaimed. "You were right!"

Each time Bryan hit the ball with the stick, we all chased after it, Brewster and the goslings and me. Casey flew over and sat on the fence to watch.

Sometimes I got to the ball first. Sometimes Brewster did.

The goslings never got there first, though. Geese are not as fast as dogs.

After a while, Dad and Bryan sat down in the grass with their backs against the fence. Brewster flopped down and put his head in Bryan's lap.

I sat down and panted. Gertrude came and settled down between my front legs.

"Bryan," said Dad. "We've got to talk about something. I'm not happy that you lied. You

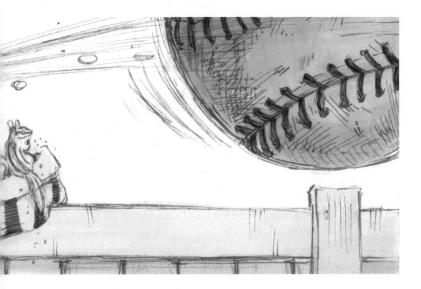

said you were going to be playing with your friends."

"I *was* playing with my friends," Bryan said. "Brewster's my friend. And Lily. They were here, so . . ."

"Bryan," Dad said sternly. "That's not the point. You can't mislead us like that."

Bryan nodded. Dad nodded, too. "I'm afraid you're grounded this weekend. Plus, you have to clean the garage."

"Again?"

Dad frowned. "What do you mean, 'again'?"

"I just cleaned it. Mom paid me."

"Ah. All right. You've got me there. But you're still grounded."

"Okay. Sorry, Dad."

Bryan and Dad stood. "Let's head home," Dad said. "I'll lock up inside."

Home! This would be my chance! I raced

across the yard after Dad and dove through the dog door into Work ahead of him.

Dad went around doing things to doors and shutting off lights while first Gertrude and then the others squeezed through the dog door and ran to be with me.

"Good night, Lily," he said.

He left and shut the door to the yard behind him.

I jumped up on the couch and put my paws up on the back of it so that I could look out the window. Bryan and Dad were walking across the yard toward the gate.

The goslings followed me. They flapped and scrambled and peeped and got up onto the couch with me. They didn't look out the window, though. All they wanted was to look at me.

My plan was working!

I jumped off the couch. The goslings

peeped in a panic. I tore across the floor. The birds fell and flopped off the couch.

I leaped through the dog door. The goslings were stuck inside!

But they weren't stuck for long. Gertrude poked her head out through the dog door and peeped loudly at me. I thought she was telling me to wait, but I wasn't going to.

Gertrude shoved herself through the dog door. I raced across the yard. Other goslings pushed through the dog door in a jumble. Bryan had his hand on the gate that led out of the yard. It was open a little. Dad was standing next to him.

I ran as hard as I could for the gate. "Whoa, Lily, what're you doing?" Bryan asked. He started to swing the gate shut.

Too slow! I was through!

"Lily! Come!" Dad called.

"Lily!" Bryan shouted.

The geese peeped and peeped. But they were all too late. No one could stop me!

I ran right through the field. I ran straight for Home.

9

Home! I galloped across the field, down the sidewalk, up the steps. I shoved myself through the dog door. I tore down the hallway to Maggie Rose's room.

My girl was on her bed, reading a book. My girl!

I jumped on the bed. The quilt bounced under my paws and stuffed animals flew off the bed as I wagged and jumped and whined with pure happiness.

Maggie Rose laughed as I threw myself on her and licked her face and her neck and her hands. I'd been apart from my girl for way too long.

Maggie Rose was still laughing when Dad and Bryan walked in.

"Did you bring Lily home for me?" she asked.

"She brought herself," Dad said, grinning. "Boy, she's smart! She got through the dog door and out the gate before we could stop her and before the geese could follow her."

"She really loves you," Bryan observed.

"That's what happens when you have a dog," Maggie Rose replied. "You get all the love in the world."

"I think Lily needs a break from being a mother to orphaned geese," Dad said.

"Will they be okay without her, though?" Maggie Rose asked. I wiggled so she'd scratch my belly.

"They should be," Dad said. "They'll be upset, but it won't do them any harm. They have to learn to live without her someday. In fact, that's what I'm worried about."

"Mom says that because the geese are imprinted on a dog, they might not learn to fly," my girl observed.

"She's exactly right," Dad agreed. "Not sure what we're going to do about it, either."

When Dad left the room, Bryan came over to the bed. He sat down and reached out a hand to pet me. I gave him a few licks to share my happiness with him.

"What's wrong?" Maggie Rose asked him.

"I got in trouble for not telling Dad the other kids won't let me play with them. I'm grounded for the weekend."

"Good thing it wasn't Mom who found out; you'd be grounded for a *month*," Maggie Rose replied.

He shrugged. "Yeah, doesn't matter. Brewster's like . . . my only friend," he said. "Ever since we moved, I can't make any new friends."

"Oh," Maggie Rose said.

Bryan sighed and left the room. My girl rubbed my belly quietly for a minute. She seemed to be thinking hard.

"Oh, Lily," she said to me. "What happens if we get the adoption fee and Mom still won't let Bryan adopt Brewster?"

That night I was so happy I almost couldn't sleep. At some point I awoke and for a moment wondered where the geese were. Then

I pictured Gertrude and Harold and all the birds wondering where *Lily* was. The thought made me sad.

I didn't think it was possible, but I missed my geese.

The next morning when I arrived at Work, the geese rushed at me and nearly knocked me over. Gertrude leaned into me and wouldn't stop, so that when I walked I was constantly bumping into her.

Of all the geese, Gertrude was my favorite. She really seemed to care about me—she would probe me with her beak and turn her head, looking at me with one eye and then the other.

The other geese all followed me everywhere and tried to climb on me when I stopped. The attention was actually nice.

For a while, anyway.

Mom, Maggie Rose, and I all took the geese into the backyard. They immediately charged into their pool. The only two things they cared about were swimming in the pool and being with me.

"I have an idea how Lily could help the geese learn to fly," Maggie Rose told her mother.

"Really? That would be great," Mom exclaimed. "The geese are old enough now that they should be able to fly. Their real mother would be able to show them how."

"You know how Casey the crow likes to stand on Lily's back? And then when Lily starts to run, Casey flies?" my girl asked. "I thought we could try the same thing with the geese!"

"Worth a shot," Mom agreed.

I was pretty surprised when my girl told me to do Stay and then put Gertrude on my back. The geese were much heavier now, no longer little balls of light fluff, and Gertrude's feet were much bigger than my friend Casey's, and felt flat, without Casey's claws.

The geese in the pool all stared in amazement. Because I was doing Stay, I held still as Maggie Rose crossed the yard. "Ready, Lily?" she called.

I tensed. We were about to do something fun!

"Lily, come!"

I ran straight toward my girl. Gertrude squawked and fell on the ground in a flutter of feathers.

"Oh boy," my girl said.

The geese all piled out of the pool and pursued me, of course. Even Gertrude, who honked in irritation. Mom followed them, shaking her head.

"Well, that didn't go so well," Mom observed.

Maggie Rose looked down at the geese. "Do they *have to* fly? I mean, what happens if they don't?"

"Then they can't migrate," Mom explained. "There are some geese these days who don't migrate anymore—they just hang around in parks or on golf courses all winter. I don't want that to happen to these guys. It's better for them to fly south."

"Why?"

"It's too cold here. If geese try to stay in Colorado all winter, they can't find enough food and they get thin and weak. Sick, too. Predators can take them very easily— coyotes, for example. They don't all die, but it is a real struggle. Much better for them to go to warmer places, where they can fatten up for the long flight back."

My girl seemed to be thinking hard. "What about if we just sort of throw them up into the air? Won't they flap their wings then?"

Mom nodded. "I'm ready to try anything."

"Lily, come!" Maggie Rose called, walking toward the far side of the yard.

I did Come. The geese all sputtered and honked, shocked that I was leaving. They made a lot of geese noises and then all ran to follow me. They didn't like Maggie Rose as much as they liked me, and they backed away a little when she came close to them. But they didn't run, and she was able to pick up Gertrude again.

Maggie Rose held Gertrude in two hands. Gertrude wiggled a little and fluttered her wings, probably thinking what I was thinking, which was that my girl was going to put the big bird on my back again.

"That's good," Mom said. "Just let her go, Maggie Rose. You don't want to throw her or anything. See if she'll flap her wings before she hits the ground."

Maggie Rose let go. Gertrude stretched out her wings and fell to the ground. She shook her head and sort of grumbled and waddled away from Maggie Rose. She didn't seem to think that Drop-the-Goose was a fun game.

I didn't think I'd like it, either. I hoped Maggie Rose would not get the idea of playing Drop-the-Dog.

Maggie Rose tried her new game with some

of the other goslings. They all stretched their wings wide and fell straight to the ground.

"They don't get the idea of flapping," Mom said. "They've never really seen a goose flap her wings."

"We could put a pair of wings on Lily," Maggie Rose suggested. "Like my fairy wings I wore for Halloween once."

Mom laughed. I wagged. I think that laughing is how people wag, since they don't have tails. "Well, maybe not that. But we'd better come up with something," she said.

"We'll figure it out," my girl promised. "Lily can do anything!"

10

That evening, Maggie Rose let me squeeze out the gate and blocked the geese, who honked in outrage. I went Home with my girl and sat under the table while the family ate dinner. This is one of my favorite things to do.

"I had to do a presentation in class," Maggie Rose told the family while she ate spaghetti.

"Oh? How did it go?" Mom asked.

"I got an 'A.' Want to see? I'll show you!"
Maggie Rose jumped out of her chair. She
hurried into the living room and came back
with a big piece of stiff white paper.

This was so interesting that I crawled out
from under the table. Maggie Rose did not sit
back down in her chair. Instead, she stood
by the end of the table, holding her piece of
paper.

Maybe this meant that Maggie Rose was all done with her spaghetti and would be giving it to me instead. That would be great!

"My presentation is called 'Why Bryan Should Be Allowed to Adopt Brewster,'" Maggie Rose announced.

Dad sat up a little straighter. Mom made a muffled noise through her mouthful of spaghetti.

"Point number one," Maggie Rose continued firmly. "Brewster is an old dog and nobody wants him. He's been living at the rescue for a long time, and it's sad. He needs a family."

Bryan was staring at Maggie Rose. He had stopped eating his spaghetti. Maybe I could lick his plate, too?

"Point number two. Brewster likes playing with Lily. And it's the only real exercise he gets. It would be good for him if he lived here and got to play with Lily more. Point number three. Bryan loves Brewster, and he would take really good care of him."

Mom put down her fork. "Thank you, Maggie Rose, but—"

Maggie Rose didn't let Mom finish. "Point number four. I got to adopt Lily, so it's only fair if Bryan gets to adopt Brewster. Thank you. That's the end of my presentation," Maggie Rose said, all in a rush. She sat down.

Everybody was quiet for a few seconds. Then Craig started to clap. Bryan quickly joined in.

Clapping is a funny noise that humans make with their hands. I don't know why.

"Well." Mom shook her head. "That was quite a presentation, Maggie Rose. But you know that the rescue has a rule. No one who works there can adopt a pet. Their families can't, either. People need to trust that we are finding the very best homes for the animals, and not just letting employees have them."

"Yeah, but you did let Maggie Rose adopt Lily," Craig pointed out. "And come on, you're a veterinarian and dad's a game warden—everyone knows this is the very best home."

"We made an exception in Lily's case, but . . ." Mom hesitated. "Bryan, I didn't even know you were interested in adopting Brewster."

Dad looked down at the meatballs on his plate. Maybe he was getting ready to give one to me.

"Yeah, I . . ." Bryan stopped to cough. "I didn't know Maggie Rose was going to do that. But she's right. I'd take good care of Brewster. And he's been at the rescue for forever."

Mom looked at Dad. "James, what do you think?"

Dad looked at Maggie Rose and then at Bryan.

"It was an excellent presentation," he said.

"I'm proud of you, Maggie Rose. Still, decisions about the animals at the rescue are up to your mom, guys. All I'll say is—Brewster's a great dog. I'd be glad to have him here. But it's Mom who gets to make the call."

"I have to set an example for the staff," Mom said. "I have to follow the rules. That's only fair."

Bryan slumped a little.

"Anyway Bryan, even if Mom said you could adopt Brewster because it's only fair since Maggie Rose adopted Lily, there's still the adoption fee," Craig pointed out.

Mom nodded. "That's true."

"That's the one rule Mom can't break. And there's no way you could raise that kind of money," Craig told his brother.

"But if he could get the money somehow . . ." Maggie Rose suggested.

"It's too much—he can't do it," Craig insisted.

Dad was watching this conversation very carefully, probably wondering when we were going to discuss giving a good dog a meatball or two.

"Bryan," Mom said. "Taking care of a dog is a lot of work. You'd have to feed Brewster, walk him, pick up his poop in the yard. Every day."

Bryan was sitting up straighter now. I could feel the excitement in him.

"Yes," Bryan said. "Yes, I know, I get it! I'll do everything."

Mom looked as if she were thinking hard. Her face was all frowny. You'd never catch a dog with an expression like that.

"I think it would be a good thing for Bryan, to save his money for something important instead of just spending it on nothing," Dad ventured carefully.

Mom nodded. "All right. Yes, Bryan. If you somehow manage to save the two hundred dollars, you may adopt Brewster."

Mom looked startled when my girl, Craig, and Bryan all burst into happy smiles.

"Yes!" Craig exclaimed.

After dinner, Maggie Rose and Craig and Bryan all went into Bryan's room. I went, too, of course. Bryan had thin pieces of paper and round bits of metal scattered all over his bed.

"I've got a hundred and thirty-five dollars," he said. "This is taking forever. I've been washing cars and raking leaves and stuff."

"You'll get there," Craig said. "I'm helping my friend Roy stack firewood tomorrow— you can have my money from that."

"And I get paid for cleaning out the cat cages at the rescue—you can have that," my girl volunteered.

Bryan looked hopeful. "Do you really think this is going to work?"

11

The days started to turn a little colder, especially in the evenings. In the mornings Maggie Rose would pet me and say, "School," and then go away, which was very sad.

Bryan said "school," too, and seemed even sadder than I was. "With school I can't do extra jobs during the day. I'm still fifty dollars short," he complained to my girl. "At this rate, I'm never going to get to adopt Brewster."

After Maggie Rose and her brothers left,

Mom and I always went to Work, where I had friends.

I was usually happy to see the geese at first, but after a while became a little weary of them constantly following me. The birds made noises all the time, like a dog with his head hanging out the window. Brewster always stirred at the honking and glared at me, as if expecting that I could figure out how to make them stop.

I was never tired of being with my girl, but a bird is not a Maggie Rose. Sometimes a dog wants to be able to lie down without geese on her face.

Maggie Rose usually came in through the door that led to the yard. She'd drop her backpack on the floor and kneel down so I could kiss her and let her know that it had been a long, long time since we'd been together.

Then we'd go out into the yard, me and my girl and the geese.

My friend Casey would come by every now and again. He'd land on the grass and take off and the geese would watch him very closely. They'd flap and flap, but they wouldn't fly.

One day Mom and Dad came out to watch the geese play Flap-Our-Wings.

"I don't think they're going to get it in time to migrate," Mom said with a sigh. "We'll have to find a wildlife park somewhere that can take them."

"Craig says they have to run when they flap," Maggie Rose said. "Otherwise they won't get off the ground."

"Probably true," Dad observed.

"Well . . . I have one last idea," Maggie Rose said. "Mom, when I call, open the gate, okay?"

I was distressed when, moments later, my girl slipped out the gate, shutting it behind her. Where was she going without her dog? I went to the gate and whined and Mom followed me but didn't let me out.

"Okay, Mom!" my girl yelled.

Finally, Mom opened the gate. Maggie Rose was across the field, running. "Come, Lily!" she called.

Chase-Me!

Behind me, the geese broke out into frantic honking. I could tell they were playing Chase-Me, too.

I ran as fast as I could out into the field. Someone had cut the grass, so it was nice and short for running. "Come on, Lily! Come on, Gertrude! Come on, Mr. Waddle-puss! Come on, Harold!" Maggie Rose yelled.

I loved yelling. I loved running. This was the best!

I looked behind me. The geese were running over the grass. They had their wings out and were flapping them, just like they did when they played with Casey.

Gertrude was in front with her neck stretched out and her feet moving as fast as she could make them. Then an amazing thing happened.

Gertrude rose up into the air!

The other geese were doing the same thing. They were flying!

Maggie Rose jumped up and down and shouted with excitement. I barked, too, just to join in.

The geese flew in a wobbly circle and then came lower and closer to the grass. They landed and waddled up to me, honking as if they couldn't wait to tell me what they'd done.

Mom and Dad had been watching. Dad was clapping. Mom was beaming.

"Great idea, Maggie Rose!" Mom called out.

"Do it again!" Dad shouted. "Let them get used to how it feels to fly!"

Maggie Rose and I ran. The geese ran after us. They shook out their wings and flapped and flew. We did it again and again. Every time the geese landed, they seemed astonished and rushed up to me to tell me all about it. Maggie Rose would gasp and I would pant and we would run some more.

It was wonderful!

I didn't see why we should ever stop,

but after a while Maggie Rose told me to do Come and we all went back into the yard. Mom shut the gate. Maggie Rose flopped down on the grass and breathed in great big breaths.

I licked her face and lay down next to her. The geese piled up around us. Gertrude didn't join in, though. She went to sit in a pile of straw in a corner of the yard.

"Oh, what a relief," Mom said.

The people all seemed happy. That's what Chase-Me does. It makes everybody happy.

Maggie Rose sat up.

"It's funny Gertrude is over there," she said. "She always wants to be right next to Lily."

"Are you sure that's Gertrude?" Dad asked. "They all look alike to me."

"Of course it is," Maggie Rose said. She got up and went over to the corner where Gertrude was sitting in her straw. She gasped.

"Mom! Dad! Come look!" she called out.

I jumped up, shoving a goose off one front paw, and hurried over to see if my girl needed me.

"Look what Gertrude's done!" Maggie Rose said. She was pointing into the straw.

I stuck my nose where she was pointing, right under Gertrude. Gertrude got up and shook herself and waddled away.

In the straw where she had been sitting was a small, smooth egg.

12

The next day, Maggie Rose and Bryan and I went to visit Mrs. Swanson. Maggie Rose carried a small sack.

We arrived at Mrs. Swanson's house and Maggie Rose rang the doorbell. Mrs. Swanson opened the door.

"Lily and I have something for you, Mrs. Swanson," Maggie Rose said.

She was grinning. Mrs. Swanson looked

puzzled. My girl handed her the bag and Mrs. Swanson opened it and looked inside.

"Oh my," she said. "Oh my! Oh my!"

"Gertrude just laid it. It's a fall egg for your collection!" Maggie Rose told her, beaming.

"Of course it is!" Mrs. Swanson said. "Come in, come in."

We went in the house and Mrs. Swanson took a small egg out of the paper bag. She put it on the shelf with the other eggs. She did not seem to think of giving a good dog anything to eat.

"How much should I pay you for the egg?" Mrs. Swanson asked.

My girl looked surprised. "Oh, nothing," she said. "It's a present!"

"Oh, no, I can't take it as a present," Mrs. Swanson said. "No, that wouldn't be right at all. I'll give you exactly what I paid for the last one I bought. A farmer found it, and he knew I liked geese, so he offered it to me.

That was ten years ago! That's how rare fall eggs are!"

"Oh," said Maggie Rose. "Well, I guess that sounds fair."

Mrs. Swanson went into another room and came back with a handful of the thin pieces of paper that Bryan seemed to like so much these days.

"Here you go!" she said.

Maggie Rose's mouth dropped open.

"But I can't . . . but that's . . ." she stammered.

"I won't have it any other way," said Mrs. Swanson firmly. She pushed the pieces of paper into Maggie Rose's hands.

Maggie Rose looked up at her with a big, wide grin.

"I have to find Bryan!" she said.

Maggie Rose ran all the way Home, and of course I ran with her. She burst into the house, shouting, "Bryan! Bryan!"

I barked, because obviously we were being loud and that was fun.

Bryan and Craig came down the stairs and into the living room.

"What's the big deal? Why are you yelling?" Bryan asked.

Maggie Rose shoved the pieces of paper into his hands. "Look what Mrs. Swanson paid for Gertrude's egg!"

"Is it enough?" Craig demanded.

Bryan ran upstairs. He ran down again with more of that paper in his hands, plus a jar full of clinking pieces of metal.

He dumped the metal out on the dining room table and spread the pieces of paper out, too. He mumbled. Maggie Rose wiggled and jumped from foot to foot. Bryan looked up.

"Well? Well?" Craig pressed. "Is it enough or not?"

"Tell us, Bryan!" Maggie Rose urged.

Whatever was going on had everyone

as anxious as I
always felt when my
girl was getting ready to put
food in my bowl.

"Two hundred and three dollars and eighty eight cents," Bryan shouted.

"Let's go!" Craig said.

Craig and Bryan and Maggie Rose and I all ran across the field to Work. Mom was sitting at a desk in the small room called Mom's Office. We burst in.

"Here!" he said. "I have it all. Maggie Rose and Craig helped."

"So did Lily and Gertrude!" my girl added, beaming.

Bryan put the paper and the metal bits on Mom's desk.

Mom sorted through them. Then she looked up. "I don't know how you did this in such a short period of time, Bryan. But it's all here. The adoption fee has been paid. Congratulations. Brewster is yours." Mom smiled.

Bryan ran out into the room with the kennels and opened Brewster's. Brewster got up and groaned and stretched and came over to Bryan. He wagged his tail slowly but steadily.

The geese, of course, came to huddle around me and honk at me as if they were dogs and I were their person. I shook them off.

Bryan knelt down and put his arms around Brewster.

"I kept my promise," he whispered. "You're

my dog now, Brewster. I'll love you for the rest of your life."

After that day, Brewster and I did Work and then he came to Home to be with us! It was very nice to have another dog around. Brewster and I could chase balls in the backyard together. When my girl was busy, I could find Brewster. He was usually napping, so I would curl up with him and nap, too, without geese.

Brewster really is good at naps.

A few weeks after Brewster came Home, Dad and Maggie Rose and the geese and I all climbed into the car to take a car ride together! We drove up into the mountains.

I rode in the back seat with my girl, of course. The geese went in a crate in the back.

"Are you sure the geese are ready to fly south already?" Maggie Rose asked. "They've just barely learned how to fly!"

From the front seat, Dad nodded. "I know," he said. "But it's the time when the geese leave, so we just have to hope Gertrude and the rest are ready."

We stopped in a place high in the mountains, near a big lake. There were geese out on that lake—big ones! Grown-up geese! They seemed restless and kept lifting up from the water for short flights and then splashing back down again.

"See? Getting ready

to migrate," Dad said, watching them. "We came at just the right time."

Dad lifted the crate down from the back of the truck and set it on the ground. He opened it. The geese streamed out, honking and flapping and looking around with interest.

One goose—she was female, I could smell—paddled close to where we stood. When she saw and heard our geese, her long neck stretched out and her head lifted.

"Could that be her? The geese's mother?" Maggie Rose asked Dad.

Dad shrugged. "No way to tell. She's certainly interested in the young ones, but we just can't know for sure."

"Come on, Lily, follow me!" Maggie Rose said.

13

Maggie Rose led me down a short path to the lake.

The geese followed me. Dad followed the geese. We all arrived at the lake, and the geese waded in. They shook out their feathers and flapped, but they didn't fly. They paddled, just as they did in the small pool back Home.

But this was not a small pool. This was a very large lake.

The geese headed out toward the middle of the lake. They seemed very excited, and looked back at me often to see if I would join them.

I don't know how to paddle. To me, paddling is not a dog thing.

I stood next to my girl on the shore. "They're doing it, Lily. They're doing it!" Maggie Rose whispered.

The grown-up bird who'd seemed so

interested in my friends was still close by. She met the younger geese in the middle of the lake, and there was a lot of honking and splashing and flapping of wings.

"That's the mother. I'm sure it's their mother!" Maggie Rose said, clapping her hands.

"Might be," Dad said. "Come on, let's give them a little space."

We went back up the path toward the truck.

A very strange thing happened when we did that.

The geese did not follow me. They stayed out on the lake, swimming in small circles and honking and flapping.

Other geese were gathering around, too. Some were beginning to take off from the water in short flights. They'd wheel in tight circles and land again. Sometimes two or three would take off together.

At the truck we found a big bench to sit on, where we could see what was happening on the lake.

"I think we're about to witness something wonderful," Dad said. "It's the beginning of their migration."

Maggie Rose held me tight.

"These geese will probably go to California, or even Mexico," Dad said. "Some head for South Carolina. Hundreds of miles. It's amazing. And they'll come right back to this lake in the spring."

And then, with a noise that sounded like a large wind in the trees, the geese were suddenly all flying.

The shadows of the geese in the air fell over us. They were honking and we could hear the sound of their wings. It felt exciting.

It felt strange. It seemed as if the geese—*all the geese!*—were playing Chase-Me, and I should play with them. But I couldn't play Chase-Me up in the sky!

I jumped off the bench. I barked a little as the geese circled, the whispers of their wings joining into a steady *whoosh*. And then some geese headed away, the sun behind them, and then the others followed.

And then they were gone.

I sat and looked up at Maggie Rose. She seemed a little sad, and I nudged her hand. Then I looked out at the lake, which seemed oddly empty now, with no geese anywhere.

I thought I understood something then.

For so many days, I'd been surrounded by geese. Geese had been behind my rump and under my paws and cuddled up into my fur. Geese had been everywhere. They had bothered me like a bad itch. I longed to get away from them.

Then we came here, where there were many floating geese, and now they were all gone and my girl was sad, which meant that the geese were gone. Gertrude and Harold and the rest of them had left to be geese with all their bird friends, and would not be coming back to Work to be with me and Brewster anymore.

And I felt a little sad, too. Now that they were gone, I realized I actually had grown accustomed to having them around. What would it be like to go to Work and not have them come running up, frantically happy to see me? It was as if I were a mother dog and they were puppies. When I was a puppy, I had loved my mother dog more than anything else. And then I went to be with Maggie Rose, and I was even happier.

It never occurred to me that my mother dog might miss me. I wondered if she had been sad when we parted, just as I was sad now.

Then I heard it. A slight noise in the air, followed by a soft *honk*. Maggie Rose lifted her hand to shield it from the sun as she looked up into the sky.

"It's Gertrude!" she cried.

It was Gertrude, who loved me the most. She landed elegantly in the water, right near shore, and my girl and I ran down as she swam over to us. She came up on shore and straight to me. She leaned into me as she always did.

"Oh Gertrude, you came back to say good-bye," Maggie Rose breathed.

Gertrude and I looked at each other. I licked her on her strange lips and she wiggled her tail. She honked very quietly.

I knew then that even though geese are birds and not dogs, they can love in their own bird way.

I heard more honking and glanced up. A line of geese trailed across the sky, all honking, their necks outstretched. Gertrude saw them, too.

With one last look at me, Gertrude turned and plunged back onto the lake. Within moments, she had lifted herself with her wings and had joined all the others.

My girl and I returned to where Dad was waiting by the truck. "Oh, Lily," Maggie Rose said. "I know you miss the geese. But it's the best thing. They'll fly far away and have a good winter somewhere warm."

"And they'll come back," Dad promised.

"And they'll come back, Lily. They'll come right back to this lake. They might even come see us at the rescue."

"And they'll build their own nests," Dad added. "Let's hope they don't pick a planter in a parking lot."

We climbed in the car. There were no geese in the crate in back. But I did have my girl. I had Maggie Rose.

And I had Home.

Home was where all my family lived. I

loved my girl. I loved my Home. I loved my family: Mom, Dad, Craig, Bryan, Maggie Rose.

Brewster, too.

MORE ABOUT CANADA GEESE

Gertrude and her nestmates are Canada geese. You can identify a Canada goose by its long black neck and the white patches on its cheeks. Male and female Canada geese look alike.

A Canada goose can weigh up to nineteen pounds. Their wings can stretch more than five feet across.

Canada geese eat grass, water plants, seeds, and berries. They will also gobble up crops like corn and wheat.

Most Canada geese live in Canada and the northern U.S. in summer. In winter, they migrate to the southern U.S. and Mexico.

Some geese who live near humans do not migrate. This can make the birds less healthy, and it can cause a nuisance for the people. A flock of fifty geese can leave two and a half tons of poop behind in one year.

It's best not to feed geese. Giving geese human food can make them sick. It can also encourage too many geese to stay in a too-small area and can discourage them from migrating.

Canada geese learn to migrate by following their parents. If a bird stops migrating, its goslings will never learn.

A mother goose usually lays four to seven eggs at a time. She keeps the eggs warm for twenty-four to twenty-eight days while her mate keeps watch nearby.

The goslings call or peep to get their parents' attention. They can even peep while still inside their eggs.

Goslings are ready for their first flight when they are between seven and nine weeks old.

READ ON FOR SNEAK PEEK AT
LILY TO THE RESCUE:
LOST LITTLE LEOPARD,
COMING SOON FROM STARSCAPE

I followed my girl across the grass to the back of the yard. There was a rocky little hill there, and out of a crack between two rocks there came a most intriguing smell.

I pulled hard on the leash, longing to get my nose up to that crack and sniff hard. But Maggie Rose held me back.

The smell was of a cat. I know about cats. When I go to Work with Mom, there are usually cats there. They live in crates, like all the animals at Work, and people come to meet the animals and then take them home.

That is what happened to me. I used to live at Work, and now I live at Home with Maggie Rose. It happened to Brewster, too.

But before the animals go Home with their new people, I play with them. I play with cats and puppies and grown-up dogs and sometimes with my friend Freddie the ferret.

I hoped I was going to get to play with this cat, even though we weren't at Work. It smelled different from the other cats I'd known. The smell was young, but at the same time, it was big. This was a kitten, but somehow it was a large kitten. A girl.

I had never met a cat like this one before. I was very eager to find out all about her so we could start playing.

"Do you think Lily can get the leopard cub to come out?" Dad asked Maggie Rose. "I really don't want to have to crawl in there after her. She's already scared. Having a person come at her like that could stress her out too much."

"Lily can make friends with anybody," Maggie Rose said confidently. She bent down and snapped the leash off my collar at last. "Go get the leopard, Lily. Go on. Go!"

W. BRUCE CAMERON is the #1 *New York Times* bestselling author of *A Dog's Purpose, A Dog's Journey, A Dog's Way Home,* and *A Dog's Promise;* the young-reader novels *Bailey's Story, Bella's Story, Ellie's Story, Lily's Story, Max's Story, Molly's Story, Shelby's Story,* and *Toby's Story;* and the chapter book series Lily to the Rescue. He lives in California.

Don't miss these

LILY TO THE RESCUE

adventures from
bestselling author

W. BRUCE CAMERON

Meet Lily, a rescue dog who rescues other animals! Charming illustrations throughout each book bring Lily and her rescue adventures to life.

STARSCAPE

W. BRUCE CAMERON BOOKS

BruceCameronKidsBooks.com

Interior art credit: Jennifer L. Meyer

Heartwarming Puppy Tales for Young Readers from

W. BRUCE CAMERON

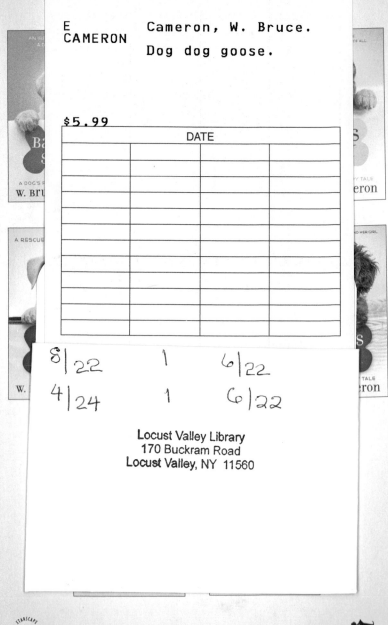

E
CAMERON

Cameron, W. Bruce.

Dog dog goose.

$5.99

DATE			

8|22   1   6|22

4|24   1   6|22

Locust Valley Library
170 Buckram Road
Locust Valley, NY 11560

BruceCameronKidsBooks.com

W. BRUCE
CAMERON
B O O K S